MOTHER'S HOME

A Novella

Ash Ericmore

Written by: Ash Ericmore

Copyright © 2021 Ash Ericmore

All Rights Reserved. This is a work of fiction. No part of this publication may be reproduced, distributed, or transmitted in any form or by any means, except in the case of brief quotations embodied in critical reviews.

ISBN: 9798844616938

PROLOGUE

Warm piss drizzled from Heather. It dribbled down her skin and dripped onto the mattress. The urine slicked across the welts on the insides of her thighs. She had been on this fucking bed, tied naked and spread eagle for God only knew how long. There were no windows, and she could only guess when one day ended and another began. There was someone on the stairs, approaching. They moved quickly.

It couldn't have been Iris.

She tensed, waiting for the door to open because every time it did it got worse. Somehow. The door creaked, the light from beyond invading the cracks and dampening the room with the glow of light. David entered. A lean, sinewy man, his skin hung from his bones giving him the appearance of an age Heather thought he had yet to reach. He was carrying a candle in a holder, his hand cupped around the flame to keep the wind from extinguishing it, even though the light from beyond was electric.

David had arrived at the house the night before they had forced their way into her bedroom. He was a younger man than Iris and he was subservient to her. He slid the candleholder onto the nightstand and looked down Heather's naked body. She pulled on the ties that held her to the bed, she screamed out through the gag they'd forced onto her a few days ago.

After she'd made so much noise. Screaming with pain.

"You're nearly ready," he said quietly, his voice

hoarse, dry. David let his eyes linger on her. Her skin covered in burns. Cuts. She could see that her broken body excited him. He reached down, his fingers coming so close to touching her, and then he pulled away, as if he remembered she was the forbidden fruit.

There was someone else.

Outside the room.

Andrew.

He came in with a perch, on which sat a crow, its leg shackled to the wooden stand. He placed it at the end of the bed. The creature was distressed at being there and it made strangled cawing sounds, pecking at the small metal cuff.

It wanted to be free, just like she did.

Then Iris was at the door. She was wearing the old red dress that she was wearing the day that Heather had started work for her. That was three years ago. She shuffled into the room, the weight of her years making it hard to walk. It was crowded there now, and Iris stood at the end of the bed next to the crow, and opened the book she was carrying. She started to read. It was a foreign tongue that Heather didn't recognise, but it seemed to calm the crow. It just settled on the perch, its gaze dropping down to Heather's body. Heather pulled against the binds on her skin, holding her firm.

David was doing something. He had turned away from her, and she couldn't see what, something on the bedside table. He turned with a syringe and stuck her just off the side of her belly. She squirmed as he pushed the plunger down, whatever it was in the transparent tube cascading into her body. She waited, expecting the drug to take her consciousness. When it did, it would be the end of her … that much she knew. This ceiling would be the last thing she saw.

Heather felt something inside her. A strange warmth released from the point of injection. This was it. It was coming.

A numbness overtook her, all the while the three of them stood and watched.

After a moment, Iris nodded to David who bent down and rested his fingers on Heather's stomach. He watched her face. Something was off … strange. Wrong. She couldn't feel his hand, not properly. Then his other hand came around and in it, a scalpel. He stabbed the tip of the blade into Heather's flesh, in the centre of the numbness.

She tried to pull away, but felt nothing.

He turned back to Iris and returned her nod. He was satisfied.

Heather knew they were preparing her for something.

David took the blade and cut an incision into her belly, long enough for him to part the flesh, for her blood to ooze out onto her skin. Heather watched. Transfixed in fear. The anaesthetic clawing at her, across and down. It wasn't until she felt the warmth on her arse again, did she realise she had pissed again, uncontrollably without feeling.

Iris never stopped reading the jumble of words.

Heather tried to scream, a dull nothing coming through the gag.

Andrew unshackled the crow, and the bird hopped from the perch to Heather's flesh without hesitation. It landed in the middle of the strip of hair she had between her legs. The things head dropped to the side as it watched her, breathing, her breasts rising and falling, as the blood from inside her drooled out onto her skin. It hopped forward to the wound and looked in. The bird shrieked and then plunged it's beak into the wound, pulling its head back out, a beak full of strings of red flesh. Heather closed her eyes. She could feel the thing there—she could feel the movement and the pressure, but not the pain. It dipped into her again and pulled more flesh from her body and she knew that she was already dead now. There was no stopping this.

Andrew came around to the side of her and stuck a needle into her thigh.

She didn't flinch.

"She is ready," he said. He was unbuckling his trousers.

Heather yanked her arms, tears flooding from her, as she watched the crow eating her, and Andrew disrobing. He was already hard, as he stood, as naked as she was, untying her feet. She tried, but she couldn't move them. She was dead from the waist down.

Andrew got between her legs.

The crow pulled strips of flesh from inside her.

Iris read the words from the book.

She felt Andrew enter her. He was holding her weight, his knees under her arse, and was fucking her.

The crow never stopped, even with his sweating, sticky frame writhing over her, over it.

David was smiling. Heather could see him hard in his trousers too. He was probably going to be next. But she was getting tired now. She looked down at the crow. For each yank of flesh that came out, it raised its head and bunted its head back, allowing the meat to slip into its gullet. It ate voraciously and without control, getting fatter without care.

And Andrew fucked her. His face contorted as he came.

Heather closed her eyes, and let the sleep take her, feeling the crow move, feeling the flesh be freed.

CHAPTER 1

"The Burns Mansion." Matty pointed across the dash of the beaten up red Mondeo, across the fields of Chainhurst to what could—at a glance—be construed as something akin to Wayne Manor. It wasn't, of course. It was just a nice, old, house that had been in the family for some generations. How many, even Matty wasn't sure. *Some.*

Brooke followed his finger out to the lush green of the Kent countryside, beautiful even with the early morning dew clinging to the top of the grasses. She looked at the house. "Nice," she said.

Matty smiled. He liked her understated way. They lived at the seaside, some hour or so drive away. Spending some of his formative youth here, Matty got away from the countryside when he was very young. He was moved to Birchingate on the south-eastern coast. He couldn't remember why, though. But that was where he'd met Brooke, many years later.

They'd been on country lanes for about twenty minutes since leaving the motorway, and were now following it around to the turn off to the front of the property. *Turn left in one hundred yards.* It was the first time the GPS on his phone had spoken in fifteen minutes and it made him jump. He indicated left and took the turn into a cheap tarmac track between two fields.

"I was expecting gates." Brooke let out a little laugh and put her hand on his knee.

"I'm glad you find disappointment funny," he

said, and then a little quieter, "Wait until you see the house up close."

The track to the house was overgrown. It should have been immaculately sculpted, but it looked like it hadn't been touched by a landscaper, or even a gardener in at least two years. Matty ploughed through the brambles that jutted out into the track without care for the paintwork on the car. The vehicle dipped and dropped as they slid in and out of potholes in the tarmac. Matty thought the track should have been gravelled. You know, classy like. But tarmac was cheaper, and judging by the state of it, put down poorly—cheaply—too. As the car came around the bend towards the house, Matty could see another car parked there.

He pulled up to a stop next to it.

Looking across Brooke and out the passenger side window, he could see that the car was still occupied. A man in a suit. He was older than Matty expected. Fifties, maybe? Matty pulled his seatbelt off and glanced at Brooke. She was looking out the window to the front of the house. "Dilapidated, right?" he asked. She shook her head, but didn't speak. He opened the door, and the cold air rushed in. "Wait here," he said. "Just until we can get in." In the back of his mind, he knew that it wasn't going to be any warmer in the house, than out in the drive, but there would be no use to them both standing in the cold for no reason.

The man in the other car had started to fuss around with something as soon as they were in the driveway. Now he got out.

Matty wasn't one for fashion, or indeed the finer things in life, but he could tell the man's suit was expensive, as was his car. It had a bonnet ornament. The man got out and shrugged his jacket closer around him. He gently closed the car door and brushed his hand down the paintwork. Matty walked over, his hand out in greeting. "Matthew Burns," he said. "You must be from Joshua Howard?"

The man took Matty's hand and shook it. He nodded. "Indeed. James Dowdry. I see you brought the weather," he said, smiling.

Matty looked up. "It should break soon. Supposed to be sunny later."

"I'll believe it when I see it."

Matty must have looked expectant, because Dowdry handed the envelope in his hand to him. A4. Thick. "This is everything that you need."

Matty took it, he gave it a glance, but nothing more. "You'll have to forgive me Mr Dowdry, but I've never done this before." He shuffled uncomfortably. "What happens now?"

Dowdry shook his head, raising his shoulders slightly. "There's nothing for you to worry about. Nothing to do. As your solicitors should have conveyed to you, the entirety of the estate has passed into your name now." He looked around, as if he was trying to find words to fill the empty space. "Any fees from your legal teams should have been taken care of, and a full itinerary passed to you. If you have any questions along that line, perhaps you should consult your own solicitor. I don't want to give you any misleading information." He took a step back, signalling not only had he finished answering Matty—without actually saying anything—but that he also desired to leave.

Matty raised the envelope. "So, what's this?"

"The keys," Dowdry said. "Paperwork regarding the things that we have been taking care of in the interim. You'll find it all in order, I assure you."

Matty nodded. No doubt. However, he still had no real idea what was going on. His head hadn't been in the right place for all this when it started, and once it had, it was no better, obviously. "Okay, thank you. Can I get hold of you should I have any questions?"

"Of course," Dowdry pointed to the envelope. "Our contact details and everything else you might need are in there."

Matty looked once again at the envelope, nodding his head. "Thank you, Mr Dowdry."

"You're welcome." Dowdry stepped forward and thrust his hand at Matty's free hand. The two shook. "Well." Dowdry opened his car door, and stepped one foot in. "I'll be on my way. Good luck with everything, and I hope that you find the house …" His words drifted off. "Anyway, please give us a call if you need anything." He dropped into the car and slammed the door, starting the engine all in a single motion, and reversed quite haphazardly around in the driveway, and then out, at speed to the tarmac, and out of sight.

Matty stood in the cold and watched him go. He shook his head. "What a strange little man," he muttered. He opened the envelope and looked in. There was a large wodge of paperwork and dropped down the side a set of keys. Only two. Matty looked back to the driveway. Perhaps he should have tried these before Dowdry had left?

Too late now.

He pulled the keys out and walked across the front of the car towards the house, waving them at Brooke as he did. She slipped out of the car and hurried over to him, wrapping her fingers around her bare arms. She made this *brrr* noise that Matty felt adorable. "Come on," he said, hurrying to the door. *Please work*, he thought. The last thing he needed was to have to call the agents and then wait in the car of a couple of hours. But the first key slipped into the lock and door opened. It was an old door, older at least than he was, but the lock on it was a Yale type. It looked new. Probably replaced by the agents after his mother had died.

He pushed the door open and while Brooke slid past him into the hallway, he stood and looked. He hadn't been here in so long. The hallway hadn't changed. Not since he was a child. That dark hard wood circular table still stood there. Where the post would sit until his father came home and picked it up. A vase in the middle of it. Roses, he suddenly remembered. Mother always had roses in it. There was a vase in the centre of the empty table now, but it wasn't one that Mother would have used. It was glass. She would have used a white porcelain one. There were no flowers in it.

"Come on," Brooke said. "Shut the door, it's freezing."

Matty shook away the memories. He stepped over

the threshold of the house and closed the door behind him with a clunk. He looked around the hall. The wide stairs in the centre of the hall leading up to a landing and the bedrooms, and his father's study behind the closed door to the right of them. His father had died years ago, and he had no idea what was behind the door now. But to him it would always be his father's study. To the left of the stairs, the living room. Beyond that the dining room, the kitchen. He could remember it all so clearly now that he was here, and yet yesterday, on the drive down even, his memories were no more than shadows.

"Still cold," Brooke interrupted.

CHAPTER 2

Matty was leaning on the table in the hallway with the paperwork from the envelope strewn over it. According to the letter that was on top of the pile—from the agents, Joshua Howard—the second key was for the basement. They recommended that the lock to the front door be changed at his earliest convenience, and that all other keys to the property could be found in the kitchen. Then there was an inventory of them. Back door. Wood shed. That sort of thing.

Brooke came down the stairs. "Sorry," she said. "It must have been the cold."

Matty glanced up. "You find paper?"

"Yes. There was one. A new one. They must have left it." She waved her hand at the paperwork and then joined Matty at the table, opposite him. "So?"

Matty shrugged. "It's all here. Utilities, council." He tapped one of the documents. "Even tells me what day the bin men come."

"You get bin men down here?"

"Private collection. Costs." He brushed some of the papers together. "It's all ours," he said.

"So what do you want to do first?"

"We should go shopping, but I suppose I should look around and check the place." He picked up the two keys and thrust them into his pocket. Looking around the hallway, he pointed to the door under the stairs. "That way," he said. "I think."

The door opened out into the classic country mansion kitchen. There was hardwood worktops across the room and a farm sink. A real deep one. A solid oak table used for the preparation of food—and for the staff to eat at. Back when the property had staff, of course. There was an old fridge freezer in the corner, old, but not unusable. Matty walked over and opened the door. It was clean and empty. Off. He looked around the back of it and found the plug. He pushed it into the socket and flipped it on. The fridge made a low hum. "That's something," he said. Brooke was at the door, watching him, but he wasn't speaking to her. Not really. He stood by the AGA and tapped the cast iron top. "This is going to take some getting used to." It was older than he was. He glanced over to Brooke. "We might need to pick up a microwave." She laughed. He tried the back door, out onto the land. Locked. Good. He looked around the kitchen. "Do you see the keys?"

Brooke came into the room and looked around the surfaces. They were nowhere obvious. "What about the drawers?"

The two of them systematically went from drawer to drawer, to cupboard. Nothing.

"Great," said Matty, crouching by the last cupboard. "Still. I can give them a call later. I'm sure there will be other things that I'll need to ask them about."

"It's pretty well fitted out in here."

Matty nodded. Pots and pans. Fridge. Cooker— he glanced at the AGA—if he could work out how to turn it on. Plates. Knives. "Did you stick your head in the bedrooms when you were up there?"

Brooke nodded. "You know me."

"Beds?"

"I only looked through a couple of the doors, but there are beds, all made."

"Maybe the agents did a good job?" He got back to his feet.

The old staircase creaked as they climbed up. The hallway was just as Matty remembered. There was still that line of carpet that trailed down the centre of the hall, but didn't reach the skirting board. The one that he had picked at when he was a kid, to find out if it was glued down or not. The walls held paintings that had hung there for years, paintings of people from the family, he guessed. He couldn't remember anyone talking about them when he was younger. He left Brooke wandering away in front of him, and he approached the first painting in the hallway. It was an oil painting, just as you would expect to find in a castle. Except the picture was nothing like one of those. It was of a man, austere, proper looking. Regal, even. He was standing with a red curtain behind him. One hand behind his back, the other in front of him clutching what looked like a parchment. Matty ran his finger across the name plate on the base of the frame. *Alfred Damelaer Burns*, it read. He looked into the fellows eyes and nodded a greeting as if the man could see him. Then he moved to the next, walking around the small table that held a lamp. The painting was similar. Another old man, the same background.

He looked in the man's hand. The same parchment. Perhaps it was supposed to be the deeds to the house? A signifier of power? He looked down the hall to Brooke. She had pushed open the last door in the hall and was looking in. She looked pensive. He followed her down and stood off her shoulder. "My old room," he said. He looked by her, in. Not much had changed, except the *him* from the room was gone. It was nothing more now than a spare bedroom. A single bed. Wardrobe big enough to have fucking Narnia on the inside of it. Bedside table. Lamp. Rug on the hard floor.

Brooke looked up at him. "So what happened? You said you spent most of your childhood living with your Uncle. Why? This place looks like a mansion. You'd be mad to leave."

Matty shrugged. He had been asked this question in a variety of ways so many times, before. Even by her. "I got sent away. No idea why. I never really had anything to do with my mum and dad after that. Then dad died and mum sort of became a recluse." He stepped by her into the room. "But I see they got rid of me pretty effectively." He turned sadly back out of the room and went across the hall to the opposing room. "Come on," he said to Brooke. "Plenty to explore. You're going out with a Lord of the fucking Manor now, don'tcha know?"

She laughed, and grabbed on to his arm, sensing his sadness. "Yes, m'lordy."

The two of them stood in the doorway of the next bedroom. "Mother's room," he said, making no motion to enter.

Brooke could feel his apprehension, and she pulled him away from the door down the hall to the next.

Matty pushed it open. It was similar to his old room. There was a double bed this time and another, large, wardrobe. "Father's room," he said quietly. "I see she emptied this out as well."

"Come on." Brooke pulled him away from the door to the next, opposite. She pushed the door open and pulled him in. "This was for?"

"Visitors."

The room was painted with a pale blue hue. There was a double bed, fresh linen. A new looking lamp, a radio alarm clock. There was a TV on the wall. "Mods," Brooke said.

Matty went over to the wardrobe, white, and opened it. It was made of chipboard. "It didn't used to look like this." The wardrobe was empty. He opened the drawers on the bedside table and pulled out a notice. It was a set of emergency phone numbers. "Maybe mum's help used this room. Nurses, maybe?"

"Well," Brooke said, going over to the bed and perching on the edge. "Then this should be our room, for now, at least."

Matty nodded. "Cool."

The two of them explored the rest of the first floor. Another couple of rooms—probably bedrooms at one time—and a set of stairs going to the attic. The door at the top was locked, and the key with the rest of the house keys—wherever they were. And finally a bathroom. *Only one?* Brooke had asked. Matty had responded by simply stating it was an old house. He remembered that there was another one in what was the servant's quarters, *wherever they were*. He was sure they'd come across them at some point. They were here somewhere. They returned to the ground floor and continued around. The living room had a fairly modern TV but the dining room was the same as he remembered. Untouched since he was a child. A long table, dark wood, sat twelve.

They went to his father's study. The door wasn't locked, and for some reason that had surprised Matty. There was a desk in the centre of the far wall facing into the room. A typewriter on one side. The desk was leather topped. The walls to the room were lined with books. His father had been using it as a library as well as an office, it seemed. Brooke dived straight into the books as soon as the door was open, but Matty walked the edge of the room to the desk. He stood behind it and ran his fingers over the back of his father's chair for the first time. Ever. It was like he was discovering a past that he had never known. A connection to a man he could barely remember.

Brooke pulled a book from the shelf and let it drop open in her hands. She gave him a glance. "I call dibs," she said. Her glance turned into a stare. "When was the last time you saw him?"

Matty shook his head. "I don't know. When I was young. Six?" It was only a guess. "I can't remember that much about him." He pulled on the drawers to the desk. They were all locked. He returned to

Brooke's side. "Whatcha found?"

"I wasn't expecting books on folklore," she said, running her eyes down the words on the page.

"Huh. No." Matty looked over the books. There was a wild selection. They ranged from local history and the surrounding area, to books on the strange and supernatural. He let his fingers walk across the titles. "The fuck?" he whispered.

"Quite," Brooke said, sliding the book back on the shelf. "I shall explore in here later. But we need supplies. Local town?"

Matty nodded. "Yeah. And I need to get the heating on."

"True. I'll take the car and GPS my way to the store if you can tell me the name. You get the heating on."

Matty agreed. He pulled two sets of keys from his pocket, the car keys and the house keys. "Head to Chainhurst village." He took his phone from his pocket. "It's gone nine now, should be open." He passed her the car keys and kept the house keys. "I'm on heat."

"Yes you are." She grinned at him.

CHAPTER 3

After Matty had waved her down the driveway, he went back into the house. They hadn't finished looking around by a long stretch, but he could see his own breath. It felt colder in here now than outside, what with the sun coming out. He supposed older places like this held onto the cold.

He unlocked the door to the basement and pocketed the keys. He had no intention of keeping the internal doors of the house locked. Didn't see the point. He flipped the light switch inside the door on, and it lit the way down the stairs. He checked around for spiders. He hated spiders.

The stairs creaked as he descended and there was a must in the air, a stale dampness. He didn't know how long it had been since the heating had been fired in the house, only that the controls were down here, somewhere. Half expecting a furnace, he flipped the light on at the bottom of the stairs and looked around. The room was sparse, a table, some furniture, boxes, old kitchenware, books, the usual sort of things people dumped in the basement to forget about. "Jesus. Fucking. Christ." He'd wished it had been a furnace. Matty walked over to the central heating boiler. "Where the fuck did this come from, the seventies?"

He wiped the dust from the controls and wished he knew more about boilers from the dark ages. He switched the power to *on*, and a deep rumble emitted from the base of the unit, suspended on the wall. He flinched back at the sound, half-expecting to be eviscerated in a fiery gas explosion. *Tick, tick, tick.* He felt the pipes. Cold. Matty pressed a couple of the buttons on the front. It was too old to have a digital display on it and there was only one predominant knob, with all the controller's indicators worn off. He twisted it around and waited a few minutes. Felt the pipe again. Still cold. Twist again. Hot water seemed to be moving along the pipe. That was good. Wasn't it? He hoped he hadn't started some catastrophic chain reaction, and made a mental note to call a plumber in the next couple of days to get it checked. Maybe get a quote for a new one.

After all, this *was* all his now.

He spun around and looked at the rest of the basement. It was going to take weeks—months even—for him to sort through all this. He had to decide what he wanted to do, whether he should leave work and move in here at the house. It was clearly what Brooke wanted. Maybe she was happy to leave work? But they still needed to work at something. This place didn't make money. That said, he had no idea how much actual cash was in the estate. He needed to get himself straight and get all this worked out.

He walked over to the table. There were papers on it. A few books. Matty looked at the titles. They looked like they might have come from the weird and strange section in his dad's library.

A door slammed upstairs.

Matty turned to the stairs. "That was quick," he shouted up at the ceiling. "What did you forget?" Walking over to the stairs and looking up he saw that the door at the top was closed. "Brooke?" he called. "Heeeeeyyy." He went up to the door and tried it. It didn't open. "Damn it. Brooke?" he shouted. "You out there?" Nothing. Maybe the wind had taken it.

Matty rattled the knob and gently shouldered the door. It didn't budge.

Maybe it had locked itself? *That's a stretch*, he thought to himself, digging in his pocket for the key. It wasn't there. Just his phone. "What the fuck?" He must have dropped it. He went back down the stairs looking at the floor in front of his feet the whole time. Across the floor to the boiler. Back to the table. Nothing. "Shit." He pulled his arse up on it and sat. He unlocked his phone and dialled Brooke.

It made a broken ringing sound. He was below the earth's surface, after all, and it didn't surprise him that the reception was a bit shot. It went to answer phone. "Hey," he said. "You're probably driving, but when you get the shopping can you come straight back? I've gone and locked myself in the basement somehow. But I got the heat on." He paused for a second. "Love you." He ended the call and looked around the room. The light lit enough for the room to function as storage, but little else. It was a good size room though. It would make a decent living space with the right lighting. But it was freezing down here. Colder than upstairs even. He didn't think that made a whole heap of sense, but it didn't matter. With the boiler down here, getting some new radiators fitted should be a piece of piss.

Matty could feel a burning sensation in the base of his feet. Very odd. He slid back off the table and dropped his phone back into his pocket. He picked up the papers from the table. They were covered in a writing that he didn't recognise. I wasn't like anything he'd seen before. The characters weren't like normal letters. He dropped them back to the table and picked up one of the books opening it. He scanned down the pages. It was old, but at least it was in English. It read like Japanese Hi Fi instructions. Broken English, talking about the dead and the afterlife. It didn't make any sense whatsoever, to be honest. He left it on the table and started around the room looking for something to pass the time with.

He opened the door of a wardrobe. It was old, but only by his standards. Looked like it was an MDF thing from MFI, back in the day. The door dropped from the wardrobe, no hinges attached. He let out a little squeal, and backed away, and then gave out a short laugh.

Matty didn't think it was getting warmer down here. He went over to the boiler and pushed his hand against the pipe, withdrawing it quickly as the heat stung him. The pipework should have given off a little heat, but he was sure it was getting colder by the minute. He rubbed his hands over his arms wishing he'd left his coat on. "Damn it," he muttered to himself.

The burning in his feet became more apparent. He paced, trying to get his blood circulating. It was obviously that. He was just cold and needed to move. The pain grew. It started as pins and needles, crackling on the soles of his feet. Then it was an aching in his ankles. It felt like he'd run a marathon yesterday. He returned to the table, the pain almost hobbling him as he moved. He sat back down, he pulled the laces undone on his trainer, and dragged it from his foot. He let the shoe drop to the floor, and pulled his sock off. The veins on his foot were more pronounced. Sticking out of his skin like they were trying to push more blood than usual around him. "Fuck," he said quietly, poking his finger down on the large vein on the top of his foot. It burned, sending a sharp, hot sting needling up his foot into his leg. "Ow," he exclaimed. "Lesson learned," he mutter. "If it hurts, don't poke it."

He followed the veins up to his trousers and pulled the leg up. They protruded in his legs as well. The pain was rising from his feet, up his shins, towards his knees now. "I'm having a stroke, aren't I?" He let his trouser leg go and wiggled his toes. They moved, but he could feel each joint with the pain of an arthritic ninety year old. The pain spiked into his knee, like someone had just Buffy'ed a stake into it. He fumbled in his pocket for his phone. He swiped his thumb across the screen to unlock it, and glanced at his foot. The veins were now darker. Almost black and pronounced. "Okay, that's bad." He pressed the call button and started to dial Brooke. He stopped himself and deleted the number, thumbing nine, nine—his leg spasmed hard—far worse than a cramp and he rolled onto the table, his leg cocked at an angle he didn't know he could move it to. "Ah," he spluttered, through gritted teeth. Lifting the phone back up in front of his face, he went to press the last nine, the veins on his arm sticking out like they were on fire, and his hand cramped, the phone falling from his grip to the table and clattering off to the floor.

He struggled to breathe.

His back curled, pushing his shoulders out and he writhed on the table, his feet kicking out, sending the papers and the books sprawling to the floor. Matty's breathing laboured. It hurt to draw the air in, his ribs stung as they moved, it was as if he could feel the blood pumping too hard and too fast through his heart. His heart felt too large, bloated in his chest. He stared at the ceiling. Tears in his eyes. He didn't want to die. Not here. Not like this.

Then it start to subside. A little. Not enough for him to move, but enough for him to breathe a shallow breath. He lay still on the table, aware of the coldness that surrounded him now. It was like he was laying in snow.

Then came a warmth.

It was subtle. A stirring inside him. It was ... he focussed on it ... the only part of him that wasn't in pain. It was below his stomach. He had just enough wit about him to know ... it was his loins. He was feeling some sort of emotional movement. *Now's not the time*, he thought to himself. It moved. He felt it pass his groin, tenderly, like a lover, then it moved out of him, away, leaving only the cold behind once again.

A stabbing, deep and hard in his chest.

"No," he muttered. He knew he had to move, or Brooke was going to find him here, like this, dead on a table.

The pain in his chest stopped, as did the rest of it. Instantly. Like a grip on him had been released. Matty drew air back into his lungs. He was still cold. He had to move, but he couldn't, not right away. The will was there, but the strength gone. He raised his head, looked at his hand. The veins were still firm and hard, but the darkness within them gone. He pulled himself onto his side, and prepared to roll himself off the table. He had to get moving. Circulate. Something. Anything.

Then the warmth came to the room.

Suddenly. Quickly. He dropped from the table, his legs unable to take the weight of his body, and he fell to the floor with a grunt. Like he'd been trapped in the snow outside a cabin and the door had just opened, allowing him to flop to the floor in front of a roaring fire. It gave him strength to move. He pulled himself up onto his elbows and looked at his hands. They were normal. He drew air into his lungs, his ribs ached, but there was no pain. He sucked it in, enjoyed the sensation.

Getting to his feet, he examined his foot. It was normal, too.

Matty rested his hand on his chest. "Okay," he said, quietly, backing up and pushing his butt down on the table. He walked gently across to the stairs and up. At the top he tried the handle and the door opened.

He stood there for a second waiting, unsure, confused.

The keys were in the lock on the outside of the door. He took them and looked at them. "Right." He pocketed the keys and left the stairs, closing the door behind him, and went to the kitchen.

He wanted some water.

CHAPTER 4

Brooke pulled up at the house a couple of hours after she'd left. She got out of the car and went over to the front door of the house. It was open. She stuck her head in and called out, "Hey. Give me a hand." Then she returned to the car and opened the boot.

Matty came to the door and out. He crossed over the driveway. "Didn't you get my message?" he called.

Brooke frowned and pulled her phone from her pocket. She scrunched her face up and shook her head. "Nothing. Damn it. Did you want me to pick anything else up?"

Matty shook his head and joined her at the boot. He ran his hand through the handles of a couple of the bags and picked them up.

Brooke studied him. "You okay?" she asked. "You look a bit pale."

"I'm fine," he said. "I got the heating on. I had a problem with the basement door is all but I've fixed it now."

"What's wrong?"

Matty shook his head and headed for the front door. He wasn't going to tell her. She'd only worry. Next time he was back in town he'd make an appointment with the doc. It was probably stress or something. Matty knew he was kidding himself, but he was a man. What was the point in having sand if not to bury your head in it? "Just a bit under the weather, I think." That would do.

He carried the bags straight through to the kitchen and put them on the table, while Brooke brought what was left and shut up the front door. "Warmer," she said. "Any problems in the basement?"

Matty glanced at her. "Like?"

"With the heating?"

"Oh. No."

She started to unpack the bags. "I've got enough food for the weekend." She smiled broadly at him. "So we don't need to do anything apart from sort out here." She pulled a bottle of wine, white, and a bottle of whiskey, cheap, from one of the bags. "But I reckon we get our room sorted out first, and then relax. We can start tomorrow."

———

The two of them cleared the lunch dishes away together, and washed up, before going upstairs to the spare room. *Their room.* Brooke pulled the sheets off the bed. They were clearly clean, Matty had insisted, but she said she wanted to be sure, and for it to be *theirs.* Matty spent the same time dicking with the TV trying to get a channel. Eventually, he managed it, and he slumped back onto the bed. His ribs still ached and his ankles felt like they had weights attached to them, but he was feeling far better.

"Whatcha found?" Brooke sat down on the foot of the bed next to him.

"Freeview. Got about fifteen channels."

"That all?"

He snorted. "I think that's effing marvellous considering where we are."

"So what we watching?"

"Eastenders."

"Fuck that shit." She took the remote from his hands and tossed it onto the rug on the floor at the bottom of the bed, before pushing him back onto the mattress. Brooke straddled his hips and leaned forward, kissing him, hard. "Well, lord-of-all-you-survey, what is it you desire?"

"I love you," he whispered back.

Brooke slipped her hands between her legs and undid his belt. She popped the button on the front of his jeans, and pulled them apart, drawing the zipper down at the same time. Matty reached forward and cupped her breasts through her shirt, feeling the hardness of her bra underneath. She pushed his hands back to his side. "Lordship looks tired. Let me," she said. She slid back off the end of the bed and pulled his trainers off. Matty gave out a little groan of pain, but Brooke took it as pleasure. Then she took his jeans by the legs and roughly dragged them off his body. "Master's getting hard," she said.

He was.

She pulled her shirt over her head, and then dropped down onto him, kissing his chest, working her way down his torso, to his shorts. She pulled them down off his hard cock and teased it with her tongue. Matty groaned again, this time in pleasure. "Oh God," he moaned. She knelt back up and pulled his shorts from his legs, before standing up and reaching round behind herself and undoing her bra, letting drop from her body to the rug.

She absently kicked the remote out of the way, under the bed.

"Lord of all you survey," she said, quietly, almost a growl. She slid her hand into her skirt and undid the button, loosening it and letting it drop from around her waist to the floor. She wasn't wearing anything under it. Just a pair of stockings.

Matty got up on his elbows. He grinned. Then frowned. "Did you go out like that?"

"Wouldn't you like to know? Tee," she demanded, making an upward gesture with her finger.

Matty sat and pulled his t-shirt off over his head. Then she gestured him away, and he slid up the bed to lean against the headboard.

She climbed on the bed and stood at the foot of it, naked apart from her stockings.

Matty could see Dot Cotton in Albert Square between her legs, but tried not to focus on her.

Brooke put her fingers on her breasts, cupping them and squeezing. She gyrated slightly, like she was dancing to some unheard pop song. All Matty could think of was the *dun, dun, dun, dun-dundundundun*, of the Eastenders theme tune. He shook his head, and tried to blink it away. She slid her hands down to the trimmed hair between her legs and down, in, touching herself.

Brooke. Not Dot Cotton.

Matty started to giggle. He couldn't help it.

"Hey," she snapped, dropping her hands away and falling to her knees, over his legs. She slapped him on the chest and laughed with him.

"I'm sorry," he said, pulling her close. He kissed her, hard on the lips, as she rubbed herself against his straining cock. "I want you."

"You'll have to wait, giggly." She rolled off him, leaving him to groan in anticipation. Brooke strode over to the wardrobe where one of their bags lay unopened at the base of it. She spread her legs a little and bent forward, allowing Matty to see her. She yanked the zipper on the bag open and rummaged for a moment, before pulling something out and holding it behind her back. Matty watched her, doing as he was told, waiting. She returned to the base of the bed and stepped up on it again. She had her Rabbit in her hand. She switched it on, the low buzzing started.

"Kinky," he muttered, smiling. Dot Cotton was staring at him, smoking a cigarette. *Oh, Ethel,* she said. It must be a repeat. Classic 'Enders. "Can you turn that off?" he asked.

Brooke looked around the floor and didn't see the remote. "No," she said. "You'd better watch me."

Matty's hard-on strained, the pre-cum slipping from the end as he flexed involuntarily.

Brooke rolled the Rabbit across her clit, holding it there, her eyes closed, her mouth open. "Oh," she said, quietly.

"Fuck me," he pleaded.

Brooke smiled. "You wait your turn." She slipped

the vibe inside her gently as she made a small squeaking noise. She pulled it out, and ran it across her clit again. She dropped down to her knees and crawled up him, without removing the vibe from herself.

As she slid over his cock, Matty felt the vibrations against his own skin. Then she pushed her heat down on his cock, the vibe still touching herself.

Matty nearly exploded as her hot, wetness slid over him but he bit it back. Kept it in. She rocked against him and it took all he had not to cum right then. "Fuck," he muttered.

"You like that," she whispered. She sounded like she was close herself.

"Yes," said Dot. "You like that?"

Matty snapped back to the there and then. He strained to look passed Brooke to the TV. Dot was talking to someone off screen.

"Hey," Brooke snapped. She got off him. "You arsehole." She let her Rabbit drop to her side. "Fucking Eastenders?"

"No," Matty said. "No, I thought ..." He stopped himself from saying anything else. It was going to sound stupid. "No, Brooke, Honey."

Brooke looked from the screen to Matty, lying on the bed, hard as stone. "Fuck," she said, again, quietly. She sat down next to him and took his erection in her hand, stroking him with one hand and turning the vibrator off with the other.

He made sure to look at her and ignore the TV. Maybe he was having a breakdown of some sort.

Still, there was no time for that. The desire was building in him fast. He was going to cum. The semen jacked out of him hard, across his stomach and up his chest. He made a weird primal grunt.

Brooke got up. "I'm going for a shower." She left the room.

Matty would have stopped her, but he hadn't gotten his head straight yet. She was gone before he realised it. "Fuck," he said to himself.

CHAPTER 5

Brooke left the shower running and went straight downstairs, leaving Matty to his thoughts. He stood under the running water, washing the spunk from himself. He just felt dirty now. It wasn't supposed to happen like that. And what the hell was happening to him, anyway? The aches in his bones seemed to have left him, but he was sure that the TV had actually spoken to him, which was, of course, utter horseshit. He could have had a mild stroke? Maybe he should tell Brooke what happened in the basement? Maybe she wouldn't believe him now. She might think he was making it up to try and fix what had just happened.

Goddamn.

They're in the middle of nowhere, where the hell do you get flowers from?

He paused. *Hold on.* He *was* lord of *a* manor, right? He finished washing and flipped the shower off. He could still hear the TV running in the bedroom down the hall. Matty pulled his shirt and jeans on and then returned to the bedroom. He pulled on his trainers and hurried down the stairs. He could hear Brooke in the kitchen, so he slipped out of the front of the house silently, pulling the door to. He circled around the house to the left, the opposite side from the kitchen window where he could have been seen, and went to the gardens.

It was colder outside now. The sun was going down on the other side of the house and the temperature was lower than it had been even that morning. The gardens on this side of the house were plentiful with wild flowers. The other side of the house had a similar garden that was overlooked by the kitchen, in which the vegetables grew. He crossed to the potting shed and rummaged around until he found a blade. It wasn't sharp, a little rusty even, but it would do. He went to the wild flowers patch and started to cut off the stems of what he hoped were pretty flowers, and not weeds. Weed. He could use some of that now. *No,* he thought. *Focus.* He didn't really know one flower from another and while Brooke possibly didn't either, the way today was going she might just turn out to be a secret botanist.

Once he had a reasonable sized bouquet he slipped the blade into his back pocket and headed around to the front of the house.

Brooke was still in the kitchen.

Matty placed the flowers in the vase that sat on the table in the hallway and took the whole thing through to the kitchen, where he presented it to her. "I'm sorry," he said. "You know I love you and I appreciate you. I just thought Dot Cotton was trying to get in on the action and I was surprised." She giggled, lightly. *A good start.* "I'm sure it's just the pressure of the house and the arrangements and everything. I'm not myself."

She took the vase and sniffed at the flowers, then placed them on the table. "I love you too." She embraced him. "But look what I found." She led him across the kitchen to a narrow door at the rear of the room. Behind it was an even narrower stairwell. "Where does it go?" she asked.

Matty shook his head. "Must be the old servant's quarters. I don't remember."

"Servants quarters," she mocked. "Your highnessness."

Matty smiled at her. "Shall we?" He gestured up, and Brooke nodded.

The stairs were bare, uncarpeted, but they didn't creak. Matty tried to picture where they led in the house. They circled up, around, and over the study. Kept in good condition so as not to bother the lord of the house when he was working, he assumed. At the top was a small hallway with four doors off it, again bare wood floorboards. There was a smell up here. Something off, maybe a little rotten. Matty pushed the first door open. A bathroom. There was a small spark of recognition. "I've been in there," he said quietly.

"Number one or number two?" Brooke giggled behind him.

Matty dismissed her, and continued to the next door. It was a small bedroom, the ceiling sloping with the roof, and with the eves of the house. It contained a single bed that was unmade. The mattress was stained. Not badly, but not made up like the other rooms by the agents.

"Do you think they even came up here?" she asked.

Matty shrugged. "No idea." He moved along to the next room. It was similar. In the eves. No windows. Just a bed. Side table.

"There's no electrics in the rooms," Brooke said.

Matty shook his head. "I wouldn't expect these rooms to have been used in years."

"Then why are the beds still here? Why isn't this storage?"

She had a good point. Matty opened up the last door. It was a larger room. A single bed still, but this room had a wardrobe, and a window. This room was where the smell was coming from.

"Christ on a cracker," Brooke exclaimed when the stench hit her. She pinched her nose and backed out of the room.

Matty held his breath and crossed to the window pushing it open. He looked out. The room was in the eves of the house but extended to accommodate some head room and a window. "Must be for the head of the staff. Butler of something," he said absently.

"What's that fucking smell?" she asked.

Matty looked around the floor. He got down onto his knees and looked under the bed. "I can't see anything, but it's stronger down here. Maybe a rat died under the floorboards or something?" He stood. "We'll leave the window open for now and I'll come back up with some tools tomorrow.

Brooke turned and went down the hall. "We should have a painting party or something."

It would help.

CHAPTER 6

Matty awoke. It was still dark. He raised his head and looked over to Brooke. He could just about make out her silhouette in the dark. He swung his feet from the bed and sat. It was hot in the room. The window was closed and he decided against opening it. He didn't want to wake her. *Thermostat.* It hadn't occurred to him earlier that there had to be one somewhere if there was a radiator. He got up and crept from the room, closing the door behind him.

He turned the light on in the hallway. Most of the memories of the house were still a blur, and he wasn't about to fall down the stairs because he was saving electricity.

He went downstairs without finding his robe. It was too hot in the house to worry about that. Crossing over to the basement door, he opened it and looked in. There was a moment of trepidation—hesitation—as he stood at the top of the stairs. The tingle in the base of his feet returned, just for a second. He shook his head and flipped the light on the stairs on before going down. He knew the thermostat wouldn't be down there, but he had no idea where it would be—another question for the agents, he guessed—so he could just turn the thing off for now. The house should stay plenty warm until morning.

At the bottom of the stairs, he turned the light on down there too.

It was cooler in the basement and it gave him some respite from the suffocating heat upstairs. How

Brooke could sleep through it, he didn't know. He went over to the boiler and turned the big knob in the centre. The boiler clicked and the fire inside sounded like it was dropping. Hopefully that was enough.

Rather than go back upstairs, Matty went over to the table and bent down, picking up the papers and books that he had managed to scatter across the floor earlier. Whatever had happened to him that morning, it felt like an eternity ago. He didn't even ache now. He was fine, sure of it. Justification done, he placed the books and papers back on the table. He padded barefoot over to the furniture piled up on the side of the room, and crouched next to it. He lifted a pin-board looking thing that covered some of the boxes.

He felt the tingle in his feet.

"Damn it," he said. Matty stood and stamped his feet, trying to get the feeling of pins and needles from them. He continued to stomp as he went back to the stairs. Maybe there was something in the air down here that disagreed with him? Asbestos? Could asbestos make you have a fit? He needed to look it up on his phone.

As he reached the bottom of the stairs, the door at the top closed. Gently. He watched it. There was nobody there, and for a split second he thought that the wind must have taken it. But it slid closed slowly and latched, just as he had closed the bedroom door when he left Brooke upstairs. He was about to start up the stairs two at a time, when something behind him stopped him. He didn't know what, but it felt like there was someone there. Watching him.

He didn't move at first. Fear, perhaps, gripping

him, but he knew—he *knew*—there wasn't—couldn't be—anybody behind him. He'd just been over there. Matty turned back into the room. There was nothing there. His eyes flitted from shadow to shadow. He felt so sure though, that there *was* something there.

The pain in his feet got worse.

He went to turn back to the door and was stopped. The shadows in the corner of the room. They looked like they were moving. Creeping like the light source was moving. Matty looked up to the light on the ceiling, like that might be moving and stretching the shadows in some way. *Stupid.* He took a step towards the shadow. He didn't know why. Instinct? An unhealthy fascination for knowledge?

A box moved. One box, at the bottom of the pile of boxes. It slid across the concrete floor of the basement just a couple of inches without disrupting the pile. It scared the shit out of him, like a jump scare in a fucking horror film. He felt his heart miss a beat. "Jesus Christ," he said. His thoughts jumped to the smell in the servant's quarters. *Rats*. He looked around and grabbed hold of the broom that was leaning against the wall. He held it up the wrong way, wielding the brush in his hand and holding the handle out like a prodding stick. He poked the box as he slowly approached, expecting a four legged little fucker to come out at him. Well, maybe. He had no idea what a rat would do. Probably run deeper into the boxes. He jabbed at the box again. This time there was a reaction.

The boxes shuddered. The whole pile of them.

Matty backed up. Shock. Perhaps a little fear. He

suddenly felt the need to piss, and he realised he was only wearing but very little.

The box tower moved, the boxes at the top tumbling to the sides, as if someone was suddenly bursting through the thing. Which there wasn't. But Matty still swung the broom handle at the approaching nothing, sticking it wildly into the air, colliding with boxes, pushing them away.

Nothing there.

Then the nothing seemed to grab him. He felt himself being restrained like there were a couple of really big guys behind him, taking his arms, maybe to *escort* him from a nightclub.

We'll do this the hard way.

It was a voice, of that he was sure, but it had come from everywhere. It was all around him. It had spoken in hushed whisper, but it was a woman. He was *sure* it was a woman's voice. Matty pulled against the force, the pressure that was holding him. Neither arm had anything there—nothing to see, just an unseen force holding him tight. "Who's there?" he asked through gritted teeth. "Let me go." *But there was nothing there.* He knew he was being held by his own madness. It was the only thing that made any sense.

Dragged around to face the stairs, Matty was pulled backwards to the table, his feet being dragged as they bounced on the floor. "Help," he said. His voice spewed out quietly. He was confused. His arse hit the table and it rattled under his weight, then he was pulled onto it. Across it. Like he was being pulled onto a gurney.

Or an operating table.

He struggled against whatever it was that held him there. It was stronger than he. He couldn't see it. What was it? Matty screamed out in fear, pain. Glancing down to his hand he could see his muscles straining in his arms as they fought. His feet kicking out, but finding nothing.

Then, pain.

From his arm. The left. Upper, near the shoulder. He craned his neck around as searing heat cut through him. His skin split from the inside of the elbow up the bicep and to the shoulder ball. Matt screamed as blood flowed from the cut, knife unseen. The skin was folded back, the pain unbearable. "Please," he screamed, "No." Invisible hands and fingers grabbed at what was inside. He saw the muscles being manipulated, pushed to the side, the veins dragged out of his body and held up like strings on a doll. He couldn't take his eyes from the grotesqueness of it all, even when he felt the same happening to the other arm.

He screamed again.

This time opening his eyes and sitting upright, still in bed.

"Fuck," he said, loud enough to bring Brooke out of her slumber.

"What is it?" she asked blearily.

Matty was shaking. His arms hurt like he'd been cramping. He could feel pins and needles in his feet, too. Sweat covered him, the sheets clung to him. "Huh?" he replied, getting his bearings. It was hot in the room.

Just a dream.

He swung his feet from the bed and rubbed his face. "Fucking shitty dream," he said, getting to his feet. He stumbled over to the radiator on the wall and felt it. It was only warm to the touch. The heating was off. He shook his head. *The fuck?* Matty went to the window and pushed it open. "I'll look at the heating in the morning."

CHAPTER 7

Brooke's friend Nancy had jumped at the idea of exchanging a few hours painting for a weekend in the country. Matty had found it harder to persuade Luke and his little brother Evan, but they'd agreed to come—even pick up Nancy—so long as he Paypal'd them enough cash to pick up some weed and enough beer to drown a horse. Which he had.

Brooke had driven off to the village again to pick up enough supplies to feed the extra mouths, and she was going up to the industrial estate on the edge of Tonbridge to pick up some One Coat to paint the servants quarters.

That left Matty a few hours to lift the floorboards in the larger room and try to find out what the smell was.

He had doubts as he waved Brooke off down the driveway.

He'd obviously gotten a touch of something. Food poisoning, or the flu. Something was fucking with his head. *And that dream last night.* This morning he had found the heating turned down. Maybe he was sleepwalking? He picked up the toolkit that he'd already taken from the boot of the car and carried it into the house, through the kitchen and up the back stairs.

Now he'd smelt the thing, he couldn't get it out of his nose. He dropped the tools at the door to the room and opened the toolbox. He took the crowbar from the top and felt its weight. It should do. Matty kicked the small rug up, flipping the corner over, and then rolled it over and up with his foot. He pushed the end of the iron in between two of the floorboards and levered one up. It came up with some pushing, shoving, and swearing. The board splintered around the nail before it came up.

The stink flooded the room causing Matty to recoil. "Jesus wept," he muttered. He pulled his t-shirt up over his mouth to fake up a mask, and then peered into the hole. He couldn't see much. Didn't have a torch either.

"Damn it."

He lay on the floor and reached into the blackness of the gap below the floorboards, feeling around. As he lay there he realised that he hadn't put any gloves on. Then he hoped not to find anything as his fingers felt around. He should stop. Matty withdrew his arm from the hole and crawled over to the toolbox. He took out the only pair of gloves he had in there. They were glass fitter gloves. Good brand, seemed everlasting. He'd never fitted glass with them though.

Back at the hole he tried again from the other side.

Matty stuck his hand in the length of his arm, knowing there and then what it was like to be a vet. He wrenched his fist around to the right and touched something. It made him lurch back slightly. After the last couple of days, his nerves were shredded. He took a deep breath. "Fuck it." He steeled himself and grabbed whatever it was. Hard to tell through the gloves but it was soft. He dragged it under the floorboards to the gap. It was light, didn't weigh much.

The stench twisted his stomach, bile rising in his throat. "Fuckin', fuck fuck." He dragged the corpse of a crow from beneath the floor. The thing couldn't have been dead that long. Its feathers had been pulled back in a couple of places, like someone had tried to feather it for cooking and fucked it up. Or—he glanced at the hole in the floor—rats had gotten to it. The patches devoid of feathers were where the maggots had started gnawing at it. Holding it at arm's length, he covered his mouth and nose with the other hand and took it to the window, still open from yesterday, tossing it out over the roof.

He brought up some phlegm and gobbed it out the window. "Christ," he muttered, getting down to his knees and looking into the hole. He lay again and rummaged around in the gap before replacing the splintered board. It needed replacing but it would do for now.

Matty sighed and rocked back on his knees. He looked around the room. This would be one of the rooms they decorated over the weekend. Sure, it wasn't part of the main house—not yet at least—but the other rooms, the normal living space, didn't have this air of cultural suppression over it.

A sudden pain in the back of his head, Matty thought someone had come up behind him and whacked him at first. He rolled forward onto his stomach and then over onto his back. There was nothing there, but the spiking sensation of pain still lingered on the back of his head. He reached up, there was a lump. It stung to the touch. Matty got to his feet. He'd had enough of this. Something wasn't right up here …

… in this house.

He picked up the crowbar and tossed it into the top of the toolbox, and closed the lid, before picking it up and leaving the room. The walls of the hallway felt like they were closing in on him. The pain rose in the back of his head again. This time it nearly knocked him off his feet. He dropped the toolbox to the floor and cradled his head with his hands. Maybe he *was* sick. He tried to blink it away. Get down stairs and wait for Brooke to come back.

He felt like he was going to vomit. His heart seemed to be beating irregularly. Harder somehow. Palpitations. What was going on? It had always been colder up here—no heating—but somehow the temperature seemed to be dropping fast. It was so cold it bit at his skin. Gooseflesh rippling up his arms. Matty steadied himself on the walls around him, afraid he was going to fall down the narrow stairs in front of him.

Then she appeared.

A woman. Young. She was smiling. There was warmth in her face as it rippled, vaporous, translucent.

"I'm having a stroke," Matty said.

The woman held out her hand. She was beckoning him forward. Matty held his chest and glanced down to the steps. Her feet didn't reach them. She was an apparition floating off the floor. Matty backed away. "What?" It wasn't Shakespeare, but it was the best he manage right there and then. "Who are you?"

The woman drifted towards him. She was reaching out to him.

Something in the back of his mind stopped him from having a flight reaction. There was something about her, something attractive. He wasn't scared, no matter how much he thought he should be.

She was ... beautiful.

She had long flowing hair that drifted in some unfelt wind. Her skin was smooth. There was something he recognised, but what, he couldn't quite finger. The woman—apparition, ghost, whatever—opened her mouth to speak, but no words came. Her motions disarmed him, he stopped backing away and let her drift closer to him. Not that he had anywhere to go. The quarters up here were a dead end.

Then she rushed at him.

Matty nearly fell backwards, stumbling over the toolbox and back to the room he'd come out of. She changed. She suddenly looked angry. She reached out towards him.

CHAPTER 8

Brooke pushed the boot of the car open with her foot, grappling to keep hold of the two carrier bags of rollers and other such peripherals to decorate, when her phone started ringing. "Bloody hell," she said, dropping the bags into the boot.

It was Nancy. She raised the phone to her ear. "'S up?"

Nancy explained that they were a little lost on how to get from Tonbridge to the house and Brooke told her that she was in the car park of B and Q in the industrial estate. She could hear papers being moved about and shuffled.

"Are you using an actual map?"

"What?" Nancy said into the phone.

"You're phone's got a GPS built into it."

"Yeah, yeah," she replied, half-heartedly, focussing more attention on the map than anything else. "I see it. Luke—" More crushing paper sounds as she talked to Luke, who Brooke guessed was driving. "Yep. We are about thirty minutes out. Can you wait for us there?"

Brooke looked around. "Yeah, of course." She stared around the car park until her eyes settled on an innocuous burger van sitting just near the road. Perfect.

Nancy rolled the cigarette around in between her fingers, giving the occasional audible tut. Brooke shook her head and ignored her. It was Matty's car and if he didn't want smoking in the car, then so be it.

She had the window open a crack and she stared out at the house as they approached. "Fell on your feet with this one, eh?"

Brooke rolled her eyes. "You know it's not like that. I was a waitress, he was a struggling artist, I didn't know that he was the Grand Earl of Dukesville and heir to the Tesco fortunes, did I?"

"No," she said. "But just sayin'." Nancy looked over to Brooke who hadn't taken her eyes from the road and laughed. "I'm just shittin' you. Are the boys behind us?"

Brooke looked in the mirror. "Yeah, they're still there. How was the trip down?"

Nancy dug around in the pockets of her cut down leather jacket and pulled out some gum, sliding the unlit cigarette in, in its place. "It was okay. They're all right, I suppose. Let me smoke in there, though, didn't they?"

Brooke didn't rise to it. "What do you think of them, though?" She gave Nancy a quick glance. "Either one take your fancy?"

"Shut your face," she snapped before looking thoughtfully out the window. "Well ..." she giggled. "Did you see that stupid Bruce Willis film the other night? He played some stupid Russian mob boss or something."

"Oh, god. Yes. It was awful."

They pulled into the driveway and along. Brooke kept watching in the mirror to make sure that Luke and Evan had taken the same turn as the two of them talked shit about aging action stars. She noted that Luke, who was doing the driving, slowed as they entered the driveway, ever protective of the bodywork of his *baby*.

The two cars pulled up to the house and Brooke got out, watching Nancy as she almost fell out onto the tarmac and lit her cigarette. *Finally*, she had muttered. It wasn't like they'd been in the car more than thirty minutes or so.

Luke got out the driver's seat, leaving his brother in the car. Evan was only a few years younger than they were, and still fitted in as *one of the gang*, so to speak. He had his feet sticking out of the passenger window and was sucking on a joint. Luke came around to Brooke. "How's he taking it?" he asked.

Brooke shrugged. "Okay, I think. He seems a bit … distant, at times." She rested her hand on his forearm. "While I've got you for a minute …" She glanced up at the house to see if she could see Matty watching. She couldn't. "Matty ever talk to you about his childhood down here?"

Luke jutted his chin out. "Not really. I mean, we hooked up when we were what, six? Seven? It wasn't exactly a topic of conversation. And when I tried to talk to him about it later—you know when we were older—he pretty much brushed me off. He fed me the same line as everyone else. *He was sent away to the seaside when he was little to live with his family.*" Luke looked up at the house. "But I never expected this. From all I could get out of him, I assumed his mum was a fucking loon, dad died young, and he was taken in. You know, like The Fresh Prince. When it came up that she'd popped her clogs, I expected him to be exactly one shitty flat and a stinky sofa richer. I didn't expect him to own Downton Abbey."

The doors to the house opened and Matty came out, arms wide, smile the same. "Guys," he called, shot a look to Nancy, "Nance."

"Don't call me that," She snapped back, grinning.

He walked straight to Brooke and pulled her close. "My lovely lady." He kissed her on the cheek.

Confused a little by his sudden bout of joviality, Brooke glanced at Luke and raised her eyebrows, getting only a blank stare back. Matty was Matty again, for the first time since they'd gotten here.

The first time in weeks.

He slapped Luke on the shoulder. "Good drive?" Not waiting for a response, he went over to Evan and knocked on his feet before reaching in through the car window and taking the joint from his lips.

"Hey," Evan half-heartedly protested.

Matty sucked on the joint. "Mine, I think." He grinned cheesily.

———

Brooke pulled the next book from the shelf in the study and handed it off to Luke. He already had a book in his hand, open. "This shit's weird," he said. "This reads like a friggin' manual. Like this stuff is real."

"Right?" she replied. "I don't know what they were up to here, but I don't like it. I want to get the decorating done and get some of this shit out of here."

Luke put the second book down and ran his finger over the page he was reading. "It says here that with the right sacrifices you can transcend the plain of death and live on. What a pile of wank." He tossed the book back on the shelf. "I get it, but there's nothing wrong with Matty. He's fine. You're fine. The house is fine. Okay, a little creepy, but I've seen a *lot* of horror films. I say we get shit faced with everyone else, smoke a ton of weed—I bought a ton with me, courtesy of the owner of said creepy house—sleep it off, paint some walls, and head back to town on Monday." He made a clicking noise in his cheek and pointed at Brooke waiting for a response.

She nodded, unsure.

"Come on." He took Brooke by the hand and led her out to the hall, as they followed the sound of laughter across to the living room. He let her hand drop before they got to the door.

Matty was sitting up one end of the sofa, Evan at the other, and Nancy was sitting cross-legged on the floor. "It's cold in here," she said.

Matty glanced at Brooke as she and Luke came in. He looked quickly to them both and then returned Nancy's look. "I got it." He stood, passing by Brooke, touching her hand gently with his as he did. She watched him go into the hall and over to the basement. He took the key out of his pocket and unlocked the door, disappearing onto the stairs beyond. She went over and took his space on the sofa.

Nancy was right, it was cold in here. Brooke looked at Evan. "So what were we talking about?"

"Well," Evan said. "For a start, the TV only has two channels." He picked up the remote and flicked it on. The screen flickered slightly as it awoke. "You have to wait a second. But get this." He pointed to it.

The picture brightened, and appeared. It was black and white. Hazy, white noise, with a picture behind it. The TV was too new to show white noise. It was part of the transmission.

"I'll turn the sound up." Evan pointed the remote at the screen.

"Don't," said Nancy.

He glanced at her and smiled, pushing the button.

The volume bar on the TV went up and all that could be heard was crying.

Brooke stared into the screen. She could just about make out an old woman in the picture, her face, framed in head and shoulders, and she was crying. Wailing. "What is it?" she asked.

"No idea." Evan turned the volume back down. "But that's all that is on the channel. I don't even see where it's looping either, but it must be. She just stands there and cries."

"Great. You said there were two channels. What's on the other one?"

Evan flicked the channel over. "Eastenders."

"Ugh. I'd rather watch the crying woman."

Evan laughed and flicked the TV off, throwing

the remote onto the sofa cushion. "So now what? Truth or dare?" He looked at Nancy, and they both burst out laughing.

"I'll go and put the pizza in the oven, if I can work out how to turn it on." Brooke started towards the kitchen.

"I'll help." Matty came back in from the hall. "Heatings on. It should warm up soon."

CHAPTER 9

They passed the joint amongst themselves, the five of them flopping on and around the single sofa. "Yes." Luke pointed at Nancy. "But did you know that when me and Matty here were at university—"

"—art school," Matty interrupted.

"—whatever." Luke moved his point to Matty, then returned it to Nancy. "When me and Matty were at *art school*, we were in a car accident, that left one of us in a coma for three days? *And* the one in said coma was moi."

Nancy stood and took a swig from the whiskey bottle before sliding it back on the coffee table carefully. "All right." She unbuttoned the front of her jeans.

"Easy tiger," Luke said, averting his eyes.

"Shut the fuck up," she slurred. She dragged her jeans down to her knees, and pointed at the scar that ran from her kneecap, up, and disappeared into her knickers.

Evan stared at her leg until Brooke nudged him. "Say something then," she whispered. "Creep."

"How?" he asked.

"Bike accident. Slid off my two-fifty doing a ton down the M1."

Evan raised his eyebrow. "Shit," he said, quietly.

Brooke slipped her legs off the sofa and placed her hand on Matty's shoulder. He was staring into the fireplace. "Where ever you've drifted off to, it's time to come back. Come on." She stood up and put her hand out for him. He took it and pulled himself up.

"Time for bed," he said.

"Wimp." Evan grinned. "Getting old?"

"Cheeky shit," said Brooke.

"Yeah." Luke slapped his foot. "Anyway." He passed the joint back to Evan. "I'm going to hit the sack too." He got to his feet and shook the sleep—and weed—from his head. His gaze moved from Evan to Nancy. "You two behave."

"Oi," Nancy said.

Evan just looked uncomfortable.

"*And* you two," Luke gestured in the direction of Brooke and Matty, before stumbling off towards the stairs.

"Can you find it?" Matty called.

Luke waved his hand back at them. Of course he could. He stumbled on the stairs, taking a grip on the bannister. He needed to be more careful mixing booze with weed. His little brother was right. Maybe he was getting old. He snorted under his breath as he made the top of the stairs. No. He was in his prime. He pushed himself away from the stairs and towards the bedroom at the end. Apparently Matty's mum's old room.

He kept one hand on the wall as he walked to keep balance. He could hear Matty and Brooke saying goodnight downstairs. Luke hoped that Evan wouldn't just sit on his hands with Nancy. She was okay. She could teach him a thing or two.

He pushed open the door to the bedroom, nearly falling over his overnight bag that he'd dumped up there earlier. "Stupid thing," he muttered kicking it to the side. He pushed up against the door as he closed it, waiting for the room to stop spinning, managing to flick the light on. "Fucking hell," he muttered. "Never again."

Luke wobbled over to the bed and sat. He held his head in his hands, breathing out slowly.

He took a deep breath and closed his eyes, swinging himself onto the pillow and lying flat. He daren't open his eyes—not at least until the weed wore off a little, and he was only drunk. He bravely opened his eyes and focussed on the light in the centre of the ceiling. He was going to have to get up and turn that off soon. He lolled his head to the side and looked at the lamp on the bedside table. He should turn that on. Then go and turn the other one off. But his eyelids were getting surprisingly heavy. Maybe he could just close them for a moment. Then do the lights.

He let them close.

Just for a second.

He opened them. The light burnt his eyes. He lifted his hand over them like he was at a match and protecting his eyes from the sun. The room wasn't spinning. That was something. Luke kept blinking as he squinted, hoping that he could get up in a moment. The back of his head thumped a little. He wondered if he had nodded off when he closed his eyes. He closed them again and focussed on listening.

He couldn't hear anything.

Maybe he had dropped off and everyone had gone to bed? Maybe without him and Matty, Brooke, in the room Evan had something else on his mind? The thought raised a cheeky smile. As long as he was careful.

He opened his eyes again as the light seemed to dim, his eyes adjusting. He thought he saw something in the glare. Something small, movement. It was enough for him to start, and get up on his elbows.

Confronted by a woman standing at the end of the bed, Luke opened his mouth. He didn't know what was going to come out of it when he started to open it. He was alarmed that someone had entered his room, sure, but she was beautiful. And naked. There was little more disarming in this world, at least to Luke, than a naked woman.

"Who are you?" he asked. He surprised himself by the quiet subtlety that came from him. She just smiled at him, reaching forward and touching his foot at the end of the bed. It was odd. He still had his shoes on, and she was … caressing them. He withdrew his foot slowly. She raised a finger to her lips in a shushing motion.

Luke frowned at her.

She rounded the foot of the bed and walked up the side of it to him. He watched. Dumbfounded. She walked slowly, deliberately. She was both elegant and, well, naked, all at the same time. Luke didn't know what to say, so said nothing. She was stunning. Her breasts were heavy, her hair was dark, long. She was unshaven. He liked that. She stopped at the top of the bed and leaned down, towards him, as if she was going to kiss him. Luke closed his eyes and waited eagerly for the touch.

As she got closer he felt a coolness on his face. A tension in his throat. Luke reached up and wrapped his fingers around his neck. Something was there, pressuring him … inside … somehow. He opened his eyes. She was there, smiling, a maniacal grin. He shouted out but all that came from his lips was a hoarse, stunted call. His vocal chords crushed, pain leeched from his neck out into the rest of his body.

She stood, still an image of beauty, but her face dowsed in sadness.

And anger.

Luke grabbed at his stomach as burning pain encompassed his body. He tried to scream. He clawed at his clothes pulling his shirt up. His skin underneath was peeling from him like it was recovering from the blaze of the sun, but with it came a scorching. Flaying. His skin started to bubble, to turn white, splitting, pus oozing from beneath. He reached down and pressed his fingers against it, and they went through him, into his flesh and beyond, destroying the skin. Pulling his clothes away from the pain as it rode across his body, brought new meaning to agony. The fabric stuck to his skin, tearing the flesh from his muscles as they cooked in place, his meat falling from the bone like a greased brisket.

Luke rolled on the bed, his flesh sticking to the sheets, blood bubbling from the wounds as it steamed in the heat. Smoking. Weak whines coming from his dead mouth as his face became an unrecognisable mush of crackling and rind and burnt sinew and cooked fat.

CHAPTER 10

Nancy woke with a start. She was still laying on the sofa, where she had fallen asleep. Evan was spooned up behind her, between her and the back of the sofa, his arm around her. She could hear him snoring, gently. Cutely.

She lifted his arm from her torso and rolled quietly from his grasp onto the rug. He didn't wake. She was hungry. She got to her knees and studied him for a moment, before her stomach growled a little. The kitchen. She got to her feet. A little wobbly—just an after effect—and kicked her shoes off. Luckily they'd fallen asleep with the lights on.

Nancy crept across the room to the hallway and out, down to the kitchen.

She pulled the fridge door open and dragged the cling film from the leftover pizza. She poked at the pieces trying to decide which one to take, before taking the plate over to the table and resting it down. She lifted the chair out from under the table so as not to scrape it on the stone flooring and wake the whole house, before she slipped into it, taking the top slice of pizza and chowing down.

The desire after some weed was strong.

Nancy smiled as the hunger subsided. She finished the slice, and then another. Covering the plate back up, she returned it to the fridge and left the kitchen. It was colder now and the temptation was to creep up the stairs and go to bed. She stood there at the bottom of the stairs looking between the door to the living room where Evan was, and the stairs, bed, and warmth. She decided on Evan. Maybe she should take him up there with her?

Evan gently opened his eyes. They were heavy. That was the weed. The alcohol. Nancy was standing over him, watching him sleep. That was sweet. She was smiling. It wasn't a deep smile, but something serene. Sedate. Her lips curled only the smallest amount. She stepped forward and slid over him, straddling him at his hips. Evan opened his eyes wider, and made a pronounced effort not to get a hard-on. She didn't speak. She just placed her hands on his chest, flat, and leaned forward and kissed him on the lips.

Her lips were cold.

She made a sound like she was eating something chocolatey and smooth and then she leaned back.

It made his cock twitch. He reached forward, cupping her breasts, smiling.

Nancy touched his cheek with the fingers on her left hand and gently caressed his skin down to his neck, inside the collar of his shirt. She did the same with her other hand, until her fingers were on his neck, swirling. Evan shifted his weight, trying to move his hardness from under her, straining, and in a little pain. Then she gripped his shirt and tore the front of it open, revealing his chest, bereft of hair. He took a sharp intake of breath, continuing to caress her. His hands and fingers explored the outside of her clothes. She leaned down and bit his nipple, just a snick, but enough for him to venture somewhere between pleasure and pain. He whispered that she was his God.

And she was.

Evan's hands quickly found their way beneath her shirt and to her skin, her flesh, cool, clammy. Her breasts firm. Young. "I want you," he muttered. "I have one, in my pocket." He let go of Nancy's breast and plunged his hand into the tight pocket of his jeans for the condom he had there, but she stopped him, pulling his hand out and placing it back, under her clothes.

"You are a feisty one," she said quietly. Evan smiled as she reached down between his legs and gripped his cock, hard through his jeans as he played with her breasts. He was fumbling a little with inexperience, and he knew it. But he didn't care.

Nancy leaned forward and kissed him again, this time more deeply, holding her mouth to his, her tongue exploring the inside of his mouth. Then deeper. He could feel her tickling the back of his mouth, and while somewhat impressed by the length and girth of her tongue, it was close to finding his gag reflex. He tried to pull back, but the arm of the sofa stopped him, the tongue now roaming like a gargantuan proboscis.

It lunged like a snake, finding its way down into Evan's throat. It stopped the air. It stopped the scream.

Evan tried to pull away from her, pushing at her, his hands still mid-fondle, before they too became entangled in something more. Then Nancy pulled away from him, back to straddling him. But it wasn't her any longer.

Another woman was there. Young. Beautiful. But different. Extending from her mouth was a tendril, an alien arm, sliding—throbbing—from her, into him. He could feel it extending, travelling down into him, probing his insides.

He couldn't breathe. His chest burned.

Nancy—not *Nancy*—this *other* woman pulled her shirt up and over her head, and where the ripe young breasts that Evan had been able to feel should have been were two arms, extending from the body, hands holding his wrists … hands with long, dirty, nails, callouses, and verrucous lesions, red and inflamed.

He tried to scream, but there was no air.

The proboscis inside him flicked from side to side, boring with the natural curves of his throat and deciding to find its own way. It tore at Evan's insides, pushing against his heart as it beat slower and slower without air. He felt the monstrous worm shoving his lungs to the side, the first of them collapsing. Then it pushed up and out. The trunk of the woman tore itself through Evan's chest plate, spewing blood up into the air, over the woman's naked body, like a geyser ejaculating months of pent-up frustration.

Nancy walked to the door, her footfalls silent in just her socks. She peeked around the door, equally wanting to grab Evan by the hair and drag him up to the bedroom, *and* snuggle back into his warm embrace without waking him.

She stood at the door and leaned her head around.

Evan lay on the sofa, dead. There was blood everywhere.

Everywhere.

Nancy screamed.

CHAPTER 11

Someone had unzipped Evan from his groin to his chin. Gashed open and bleeding still, his corpse twitched feverishly. He was still on the sofa. His clothes torn open, much like his skin. His insides, guts, spewed from the wound and blood pooled in a circle emanating out from the sofa like someone had dropped a bottle of cherryade on the rug. But it didn't stop there.

Whatever had done it had made a mess. The blood and gore splattered from the body, across the room, on the walls. Even some on the ceiling. It looked like a Lovecraftian crime scene.

Nancy's scream had roused Matty and Brooke. The two of them bounded down the stairs to her side. She just stood there at the doorway, staring in at Evan, her hands over her mouth.

Matty came by her and stood at her side. He stared at the body, as Brooke took Nancy in her arms. "What is it?" Brooke asked. She hadn't seen. She hadn't looked.

Matty took a small step back. He wanted to ask what had happened but the words weren't there. There was nothing there except for the feeling of sickness that rode over him. Then the thought of Luke came to his mind. He turned around a looked up the stairs half expecting him to be standing there. Thankfully he wasn't. Maybe he hadn't heard Nancy's scream. Matty turned to Nancy. He took her by the shoulder, pulling her from Brooke's arms.

"What happened?" he asked. She just stared at him, and a sudden wave of anger broke out of him. He squeezed her shoulders, digging his fingers into her flesh. "What the fuck happened?" he asked again, this time harsher, accusingly.

She tried to wriggle free from his grip.

Brooke tried to pull him off. "Hey," she said, a voice of reason. Quiet. Sincere.

Matty pushed her away, before returning his attention back to Nancy. "Tell me." He let go of her shoulders and shoved her into the door frame. Her head bounced off the wood with a *thunk*.

"What the fuck?" Brooke got between them. "What are you doing?" She shot a glance over to Evan. To his corpse. She let a sharp intake of breath be her only action before taking Nancy by the arms and leading her away from Matty's reach. "What happened?" she asked her quietly.

Nancy was sobbing. She was shaking uncontrollably like hypothermia was kicking in.

Matty approached Evan. The smell of blood, iron, it overtook the room, was nauseating. He held his hand over his mouth. What should he do? Check his pulse like they did in the films or something. He stepped back as the blood pooled further out from the sofa. There was no point, he realised. He turned and glanced at Nancy and Brooke. They'd moved over and were sitting on the stairs, Nancy crying uncontrollably into Brooke's shoulder. Matty stepped passed them onto the stairs.

"Where are you going?" Brooke asked quietly.

"I left my phone in the bedroom." He stopped and looked up the stairs. "And keep your voice down. I don't want to wake Luke."

Matty took off up the stairs two at a time. He was bare foot, and moving quietly was easy. Glad to get away from the smell, he used the time alone to think. He'd never seen anything like it. Surely Nancy couldn't have done it? Sure, she was stoned off her block when they went up to bed a couple of hours ago, pissed as a fart, but there was no way she was capable of that. He paused at the top of the stairs and looked over the bannister to Brooke, still comforting Nancy. He suddenly didn't want to leave her there with Nance. Just in case. He looked down the hall to the room Luke was asleep in. No. He had to get his phone and the police here as soon as possible. If Luke awoke and saw that, who knew what he might do.

Matty went along the hallway and ducked into his and Brooke's room. He slid the door shut and went over to the bed, sitting. He took in deep breaths, picking his phone up from the bedside table and holding onto it like a lifeline. He realised that he was shaking as well. *Police*, he said in his head, over and over. It occurred to him that in all these years he'd never actually called *999*. Swiping the phone to bring up the keypad, he punched in the code to unlock it.

"Stop."

A woman's voice. It made it his heart miss. "The fuck," he said, quietly.

"Language," she snapped.

Matty looked up over the lip of the phone and to Iris, standing there in front of the door, still closed.

"Mum." The words floated from his lips like he hadn't really said them. "Mum," he repeated at he stared at her. She was how he remembered her, at least, through the fog that clouded time. Memories from so many years ago.

She smiled. "Matthew Leon Burns," she said. "You've grown."

Before he knew what he was doing he replied, "Matty. It's Matty these days."

"Son," she said, crossing the room to him.

He withdrew instinctively. "Who—" He stopped himself from asking. He could see who she was. It was just impossible. He realised he still had the phone in his hand and had only dialled the first two numbers. She put her hand across the phone and pulled it gently from his hands. He could have stopped her. There was no force in the gesture, but he wasn't of the mind.

"No," she said. "You need to stay here with me." She leaned forward and kissed him. It began tenderly on the lips, a mother touching a son that she hadn't felt the warmth of in time, then it became harder. She was forcing herself onto him.

Matty tried to pull away, but she had placed her hand around the back of his neck, holding him tight.

Her tongue pushed against the lips of his closed mouth.

He grunted, groaning, trying to object, that she was pushing too hard, but his fight pushed her forward, her determination growing. She managed to part his lips, her tongue feeding into his mouth, raping it. With no other choice he swung he fist into her gut. She took it like a champ, barely flinching with the blow.

She opened her eyes and looked into his. He could see the joy in them. He could see that she was getting what she wanted as she invaded him. She pulled away, long enough for him to take a breath.

"Come to mummy," she said, quietly. Seductively.

She was on him. Over him. He could feel her touching him as she crawled on him, pushing him back onto the bed like a desperate lover. She forced her lips onto his again, pulled at his clothes. He tried to push her off but she had the strength of eleven men. He punched at her, and clawed. He couldn't breath with her pushed up on him like this. He had to get away. His chest was starting to hurt.

And then as quickly as she had appeared in the room, she was … in him. Invading him. He couldn't move. Speak. Pain raptured across his face as he felt his mind shrinking into himself. His feet … he could feel the blistering pain moving up them again, overtaking his body like he was stroking out … but that wasn't all …

He was changing.

CHAPTER 12

Brooke moved her head away from Nancy, and looked up the stairs when she heard movement, praying it wasn't Luke. Matty stood on the landing. He was looking down at the two of them. Nancy was still weeping. Brooke frowned at him, trying to ask him silently what was going on, but it seemed the meaning in her look was lost on him. He returned her look, staring into her eyes, but gave no meaning in it, before starting down towards them.

Brooke looked from his one hand to another. "Where's your phone?" she hissed, as if Nancy wouldn't hear. Nancy didn't move from her position.

Matty walked by them, into the hallway and across towards the front door.

"Matty," Brooke snapped. "What's going on?" It was like he was spaced out. Monged on something stronger than weed. Shock perhaps?

He pulled the front door open and looked out into the night, facing away from them. Brooke could see him moving, breathing. Then he turned back to them. "Get out," he said.

Brooke just stared at him, and Nancy looked up, acknowledging him for the first time since he returned down the stairs. "What's he talking about?" she wheezed, snot running from her nose and onto her lips.

Matty just stood there, holding the door. Finally he gestured as a doorman would. *Out you go.*

"What the fuck is wrong with you?" Brooke shouted at him. "Look at him," she said, pointing into the living room. "We need to call for help."

Matty left the door open and crossed to the doorway. He looked at Evan and nodded. "One of my finer works." He spun on his heal back to face the door, and marched out of it, with one finger held up in some sort of eureka motion. He disappeared out into the night.

Brooke let Nancy nestle her head back into her shoulder. "What the fuck was that?" she asked. Brooke watched the door silently.

Shortly, maybe three minutes later, Matty returned. He was dragging an axe behind him. Brooke immediately shook Nancy off her and stood, as Matty raised the axe up, his hand on one end of the hilt the other holding the wood just below the blade.

"What's that for?" Brooke asked quietly.

Matty bounced the axe like he was weighing it up in his grip. "Get the fuck. Out."

"This isn't funny." Brooke looked around, confused, pulling at Nancy's arm at the same time to get her up.

Matty caressed the hilt of the axe. "I said, get the fuck out of my house." He didn't wait for a response this time. "Actually," he continued. He raised the axe up as it he was going to chop wood. "It really doesn't matter." He brought the axe down, slamming it into the floor, carving through into the wood, cleaving the rug apart. He was nowhere near Brooke and Nancy, but that didn't stop Nancy from screaming the house down. Brooke dragged her up to her feet and started to back up the stairs, still facing Matty.

"What are you doing?"

Matty was busy yanking on the handle of the axe, muttering under his breath, trying to release it from the floorboard.

Nancy finally seemed to get her shit together enough to let go of Brooke and become something less of a burden. She was up, under her own weight and standing next to Brooke on the stairs. "I don't like this," she said between sobs. "Let's go."

Brooke nodded slowly as Matty got the axe from the floor and looked back up to the two of them. He had a look in his eyes, one that Brooke had only seen on him when she was naked. He was hungry. Only this time, she wasn't sure what he was looking at eating. She turned back on the stairs and ran upwards, grabbing Nancy by the elbow and towing her up. "Come on," she barked.

Nancy charged up the stairs behind her and the two of them hit the landing running. "In there." She pointed to the last room on the right. "You take that one, I'll take this one." She leaned up against the door on the left and watched the stairs as Brooke ran down to the last door. She opened it and gave a glance to Nancy. They nodded quickly and both disappeared into their respective rooms to hide.

CHAPTER 13

Nancy closed the door behind her slowly enough that it wouldn't be heard. She could see the shadow cast by Matty as she did, as it loomed up the stairwell on the wall. The door latched, she turned into the room. It was the bathroom. Great. She should have thought more about this.

She fumbled with the latch. Broken. *Fuck*.

Over at the sink she opened the medicine cabinet door. Nothing of use. She picked up Matty's safety razor. It looked like he'd been using the same one for years. It wasn't going to cut butter. She dropped it into the sink. There was a creak of a floorboard. He was in the hallway outside the door.

Nancy shrunk into the corner. She looked into the toilet bowl below her. Floater. Fucking hell. She picked up the safety razor. It was better than nothing.

She waited.

The knob twisted, the door creaking as it opened. Matty pushed the door inwards, opening it towards her. Nancy looked him straight in the eyes.

He looked different.

He looked like someone else.

She raised the razor like a knife and screamed as she charged at him. Letting out an, "*Ahhh*," that would have put William Wallace to shame, she burst across the room intent on impaling him with the plastic handle, if nothing else.

Matty looked a little surprised as she started. But he seemed to shake it off pretty sharp, as she got within reach, he wrenched his elbow around snatching her on the upper arm hard. Hard enough to knock her from her feet.

Nancy, half pushed, half slipping on the tiled floor of the bathroom, trunked arse over tit into the bath. She cracked her head on the tiles and her shoulder made a strange sound not unlike the sound of someone chewing gristle as it moved into an awkward and considerably painful angle. "Fuck," she screamed, rolling onto her back. Matty was standing over her looking at her like someone watching a puppy falling down stairs. Pity, mixed with humour. She stabbed up toward his head with the razor still held firmly in her grip. She collided with the side of his head, causing him to tumble—a little—to the side. She looked down at the razor, which had snapped in half. She tossed the half of it away that she still held and pulled herself up to her feet as Matty regained some composure.

"Bitch," he said.

"Cunt," she riposted. She lunged from the bath, arms out like Superman, and grabbed hold of Matty, knocking him backwards, and for a split second, the thought of getting out of this in one piece crossed her mind.

Matty crashed into the door, his head bouncing off the hardwood. He let out a sound like a shit horror movie scream queen.

Nancy flailed, trying to keep her footing, but fell forward, onto her knees on the bathmat. She felt her knees go. That weakness that bones got when you drank too much and smoked too much? Even at her age she was afflicted, and when her knees took her weight she knew that she wasn't getting up. A burning hotter than Hell itself fired across her legs as her kneecap on the left leg spun out of place. She looked down as saw the bone jutting out to the side as the pain flared to an unbearable level. At least the bone wasn't sticking out of her skin. Right? She looked up to Matty as he straightened over her.

He still held the axe firmly.

Nancy looked at the door. Maybe Brooke had heard her scream of attack and was coming to help, bursting into the bathroom around the corner at the last second to save the day.

Brooke wasn't there.

She looked back up at Matty, stood over her smiling, his legs spread wide as he got his balance. He was caressing the axe handle as he lifted it like he was standing over firewood. Nancy sighed. At least it was going to be quick.

Matty slammed the axe down as hard as he could.

He missed Nancy's head, which is what she had assumed was going to be her last thought. *He's going to axe me in the head.* She was right. Her head was his intended target, but he missed.

The head of the axe slid through Nancy's clavicle, the sheer weight of it driving it through to the muscle and down, sliding out of the body with no control. Then her arm fell off. Blood gushed from her shoulder as her body crumpled to the floor. She would have put her arm out to stop herself, but, well, you know. Nancy lost consciousness soon thereafter.

Shock.

Matty turned and stalked out of the bathroom. He kicked Nancy's arm without thought as he passed, but it rolled out of the door, into the hallway and onto the carpet. Like a beer can kicked by a kid in the street. He nodded at it, and turned back down the hall.

CHAPTER 14

Brooke had nodded to Nancy and slid backwards into the room, before closing the door as quietly as she could. She leaned her forehead against the wood as she tried to think. She needed to get out of the house. She turned into the room and her eyes fell on Luke, lying half on the bed and half on the floor. She had completely forgotten about him. He was dead.

Of course he was.

He looked like chopped fucking liver. How had anything done that to him without them hearing?

Brooke put her hands over her mouth as if to stifle a scream, but as with Evan being butterflied downstairs, seeing Luke lying there in a similar way, she didn't find it that bad, really. She let her hands drop from her mouth and approached him. She got close enough to be sure that he was dead, and then turned back to the door.

There was a scream.

Brooke reached for the door handle and then thought twice about it. What if Nancy was in trouble? There was an angel on her shoulder screaming out for her to open the fucking door. She grabbed the handle and pulled the door inwards, sticking her head out into the hallway in time to see an arm roll across the floor on the carpet. "Fucking hell," she whispered, slipping her head back into the room. She held the door closed and glanced around for a weapon. Nothing of much use. She ducked down and pulled open the bag on the floor. Luke's. She grabbed the only thing in it that might have been any use. A twelve inch glass bong. She held it like a short sword. It would have to do. She pulled the door open and burst into the hallway, startling Matty, judging by the look on his face. He was stood in the centre of the hallway with the axe in one hand casually slung over one shoulder. "What the fuck do you *want*?" she screamed at him.

He shook his head. "Me? This is my house you wretched shit squirting whore." He smiled coyly and raised his free hand over his lips. "Sorry," he said. "Do forgive my candor."

Brooke looked weak. "Matty," she said, pitifully.

"Matty?" Matty shook his head. "Oh no, my dear. Matthew has taken his leave. I'm his mother."

Brooke dropped her head down to one side. "Well aren't we a bitch?" she asked.

"You foul mouthed money chasing daughter of a pig."

"Better a pig's daughter than a cunt."

Matty wrinkled his nose up. "You girls keep saying that. It's disgusting."

Brooke lifted the bong above her head and charged with a war-cry to match that of Dutch fighting a predator. Matty again looked surprised. He had barely managed to get the weight of the axe from his shoulder, overestimating his strength, when Brooke reached him. She drove the bong into his face. It was a blow out of desperation and she did regret it.

But needs must.

The thick glass shattered, knocking Matty from his feet, shards of broken glass sticking out from his flesh, the weight of the axe helping to take him over. Brooke went to run, but paused. She turned the bong around like a stake and thrusting it downwards to impale Matty where he lay.

Matty rolled off to the side, frantically swinging the axe in his hand, the bong never landed its target. Instead, Matty managed to knock Brooke from her feet. She wailed as she struggled back to stand. Anger rushed through her.

Matty fought to try to get to his feet.

Brooke weighed up her options, and frankly, they were all shitty, so she hurled the broken bong at Matty and ran passed him to the stairs and started down. Matty brushed the bong away as shards of glass bounced harmlessly from him and he charged down the hallway after her.

"Fuck it. Fuck it. Fuck it," Brooke mantra'd as she shot down the stairs, Matty close on her heals. She glanced at the open front door, quickly deciding that she wasn't going to be able to outrun him, especially not outside. Plus it was dark. Pitch black away from the light of the house. She held onto the knob on the end of the bannister and hurled herself around it. She could hear Matty's feet as they thudded against the stairs.

He was so close.

Brooke crashed through the closest door. On to the basement stairs. She mashed her hand on the light switch but didn't manage to flick it, so she kept moving in the dark. Downwards, slamming the door behind her, but not even stopping to see if she could lock it or stop him from coming through in any way. She plunged through the blackness, nearly leaving her feet when she reached the bottom of the stairs and she hit the flat concrete floor, unseen. She turned, flailing in the dark.

Then light gushed down from the doorway as Matty opened it. The light from the hallway beyond first, and then the light as Matty turned on the light switch. "You damaged my baby boy's face," Matty said.

Brooke could hear him coming down the stairs toward her. Two steps followed by a pronounced *thunk*.

She looked around the basement. There was little weapon-wise. Furniture. Brooke's eyes fell on the pile of kitchen equipment. She ran over and grabbed the first thing she saw. Two handles and a rusty curved blade between them. Some sort of herb cutter from before the war. The one with the Roundheads by the look of it. She turned and faced the stairs, the shadow of Matty looming across the floor. He reached the bottom of the stairs and looked at her, holding the axe behind him where he had dragged it down the stairs. "Matty, baby, you gotta fight this. You gotta come back to me."

Matty shook his head, looking up to the ceiling of the basement with some awe in his look. "It is not that simple, whore. This house, *this house*, this is what has your beau. Not me. Not this old woman. But the house. The family home. It was Matty's father's fault, I think, but that was so long ago. When he was dabbling in the occult," he said quietly. He looked at the floor, dismayed. "It was when I sent him away. To live with my sister. She understood, but she never said anything. And then George ..." He looked up and met Brooke's gaze. "... Matty's father—he did something to make the house want to live through the family. I tried to keep him away. I thought it would die with me. But it didn't. You've seen The Exorcist, right?"

Brooke was taken aback by the sudden question, shrugging a vague agreement.

Matty nodded. "Normally you see a change in the physical being and the mind is taken over by something inherently evil, but in this case the house wouldn't let me die and I ..." He looked to the side, there was regret in his face. "... I brought back something on my shoulder. Something evil." He looked back to Brooke. "And I can't control ... me."

"So he's not in there anymore?"

Matty shrugged, sticking his bottom lip out. "No fucking idea. But we'll not find out."

Brooke broke into a run without warning, charging at Matty with him still holding the axe to the floor. "*Fucker!*" she screamed, waving the herb cutter at him like her life depended on it. Which it did, really.

She smashed the rusty blade into Matty's arm as he fought to lift the axe, still unsure of his own capabilities. The ancient blade was still true and it slashed deep into his flesh without effort. He yelled out, grabbing at his arm and falling backwards, onto the stairs. Brooke trampled him to get to the top of the stairs, smashing her foot into his face. She heard the cracking of what she expected was his nose breaking. Maybe teeth.

He cried out again.

Brooke charged up the stairs and out into the hallway. She slammed the door behind her. The key was in the lock. She turned it and slipped it out into her pocket.

"Bitch," the voice came from behind the door. "Let me out." The handle rattled.

"Fuck that, and fuck you." Brooke backed away from the door. "It's this fucking house, you say?" She left the hallway going into the living room, ignoring Evan's desecrated body on the couch, and going over to the log fire. She scooped up the packet of matches in the hearth. "Fuck this house," she muttered.

Brooke ran upstairs to hers and Matty's bedroom and retrieved the car keys, before returning to the ground floor. She went into the kitchen and turned the gas on, on the AGA, letting the vapour flow freely into the room.

Then she went across the hallway to the study.

She could hear Matty banging on the door, hard. He wasn't getting through though. She crossed to the bookcase and started pulling books from the shelves, creating an unlit bonfire pyre on the floor. Once it reached a reasonable level, she took the matches and lit one, resting the flame against the flopped open pages of the books—books used to create the inorganic life that now lived by the house, in Matty. She could hear him screaming as the fire took.

Brooke got out of the house and into the Mondeo.

She started the engine and pulled away, into the darkness of the driveway.

The car rode from side to side, sliding off the bushes, barely staying in a straight line, as the first explosion rocked it. Brooke slammed her foot onto the brakes and the car slid to a halt. She looked in the mirror at the house, a raging bonfire, as flames licked from the windows on the ground floor, from the open front door.

She watched, waiting to see if Matty was going to run from the flames.

About the Author

Ash is a British horror author. He resides in the south, in the Garden of England. He writes horror that is sometimes fantastical, sometimes grounded, but always deeply graphic, and black with humour.

Printed in Great Britain
by Amazon